We Are Family ~Bing

WELCOME TO
★ FORT ★
GOODE

WRITTEN BY **WINSOME BINGHAM**
ILLUSTRATED BY **COLIN BOOTMAN**

To: Zetarius D. Hambrick and veterans near and far, thank you for serving your country, fighting for our freedom, and defending our liberties.

And to all the children of military servicemembers, thank you TOO for your service.

Reycraft Books
145 Huguenot Street
New Rochelle, NY 10801

Reycraftbooks.com

Reycraft Books is a trade imprint and trademark of Newmark Learning, LLC.

Text © Winsome Bingham

Library of Congress Control Number: 2022915665

Hardcover ISBN: 978-1-4788-7585-7
Paperback ISBN: 978-1-4788-7586-4

Photo Credits: All images from Shutterstock and Getty Images.
Author photo: Courtesy of Winsome Bingham
Illustrator photo: Courtesy of Colin Bootman

Printed in Dongguan, China. 8557/0223/19867
10 9 8 7 6 5 4 3 2 1

First Edition published by Reycraft Books 2023.

TABLE OF CONTENTS

GOODE-BYE OLD

Lang Ford and his family said goodbye to their old post.

They were moving again.

His dad PCS-ing, Permanent Change of Station,

from one military post to the next.

They were leaving their old post behind.

Their community.

Their work and school.

Their home.

And Lang was leaving his friends, which he wasn't happy about.

They had been driving for a long, long time.

From sunlighty day to dark starry night to sunlighty day again.

Their new home was in Virginia.

Lang pointed at the sign.

He scooted closer to the window. "Is this it, Dad? Are we here?"

His dad pulled up to the checkpoint and stopped. "We're here, son. We're home."

He rolled the window down,

dug into his wallet,

and pulled out his ID, a military identification card.

An MP walked up to the car.

Her weapon slung across her back.

"ID, please," she said.

"Sergeant First Class Ford reporting for duty," he said and handed her his ID.

First, she scanned the bar code on the front.

Then she looked at the picture,

looked at him,

looked at the picture again,

and handed it back.

She was making sure Lang's dad was who he said he was.

Lang rolled his window down and handed her his ID. "I'm Lang."

"Hi, Lang," she said taking the ID.

She looked at the picture,

looked at Lang,

looked at the picture again,

and handed it back.

Lang pointed at his mother.

"And that's Momma. She's a scientist."

"Now, baby, the woman didn't ask you all my business," said Momma.

The MP smiled and nodded. "Ma'am."

Lang's momma smiled, nodded, and gave up her ID.

The MP did the same with momma's ID as she did with the rest.

Then she handed back the ID,

gave them a map,

and said, "Welcome to Fort Goode."

THE GOODE HOUSE

Lang's dad drove slowly,

passing barracks and boats,

tanks and trucks,

chinooks, cargo carriers, and combat vehicles.

He waved at the motorpool. "See you next week."

He turned on Armstrong Street and parked in front of a two-story house

with its reddish-brown bricks, a red door with a gold knocker, and big bay windows.

The yard had a table with benches in the middle of the lawn.

Lang shoved his head out the window. "Is this it?"

His mouth slowly opened. "Wow!"

"Another home to fall in love with and then leave," Momma said.

Dad looked at Momma.

She quickly turned her head,

stepped out of the car,

and shut the door. *SLAM!*

Dashing up the driveway,

Lang sprinted across the lawn,

up the steps,

across the porch,

and tugged on the locked door.

He walked around the wraparound porch.

He pressed his face against the window,

and peeked inside the empty house.

"You're going to love it here," said Dad.

"Hmm-hmm. Another home to fall in love with then leave," said Momma.

Dad looked at Momma.

She shrugged.

Her hands up, palms facing the sky. "What?"

He shook his head.

Lang raced to the end of the driveway and looked up the street.

"There's no bodega. I want the bodega."

"There's a 7-11. And I'm sure they sell sandwiches," said Momma.

Lang looked down the street.

"What about the basketball court? We just got a new blacktop and backboard."

"We're not far from a golf course," said Dad. "Maybe it's time we learn golf."

Lang leaned against the fence. "I want Corporal Coop cutting my hair."

"It doesn't matter who cuts your hair. Just as long as you get a haircut," said Dad.

"I want home," Lang said. "I want our old home and my old friends."

Lang's dad glanced at his momma. "You're up."

Momma took Lang's hand, and they walked over to the bench and sat.

Dad followed them.

"Now, listen here," she said, taking his face in her hand. "You are home, baby. This is home. Our home."

"That's right, son," Dad said. "Your home is with me and your momma. Wherever we are, that's home."

"Your daddy is right. This is it for now. We will fall in love with this one just like we did with the last. And the last before that. And the last before that. And if we must leave again, we will do what we always do. We will pack right on up. And keep on moving. But as long as we together, we home."

Tears rushed down Lang's cheeks. "You don't even like it here," he said.

"Wait, what?" asked his momma.

Dad looked at Momma.

"Listen," she said. "I never like it when we first move. That's because I miss my friends and my job and the hospital. At first, I didn't like our last post either. But after a while, I grew to love it. And the same thing will happen here. It takes time. And you will be fine. We will all be fine. We will be good at Fort Goode."

Lang hugged his momma. "You're one great momma."

"And you're one great son. Now take the keys from your daddy and let us in our new home."

Dad handed Lang the keys and he hotfooted across the lawn,

up the steps,

across the porch,

and opened the door.

"We're home," he screamed.

"You're one great wife," Dad said, kissing Momma on her cheek.

"And you better not forget it," she said.

"Let's go home," he said.

GOODE FRIENDS

Lang had been at Fort Goode for more than a week, and he was still missing his old home,

his old post,

his old friends.

Fort Goode was quiet.

No early morning traffic. **Honk-honk-honk!**

No early morning sounding off. **Hoo-rah!**

No early morning soldiers sprinting while singing— **"Hey, hey Cap'n Jack, meet me down by the railroad track..."**

Lang loved the ***Honk-honk-honk!***
and the ***Hoo-rah!***
and the ***"Hey, hey Cap'n Jack, meet me down by the railroad track..."***

Most importantly, he missed his friends.

Three children strolled up the driveway.

One girl carried a skateboard in her hand.

Two boys rode bikes.

The girl waved at Lang. "Hi."

The boys waved too.

"Hi," said Lang, walking down the driveway.

"I'm Ying," she said.

"I'm Carlos," one of the boys said.

The other boy pointed at Carlos. "I'm his brother, George."

Lang waved at them. "I'm Lang."

"We're going to the park," Ying said. "I'm going to skate. The bros are going to ride."

"The bros are us," George said.

He gently shoved his brother, Carlos.

"I think he knew that," said Carlos.

"You don't know that he knew that," said George.

Carlos rolled his eyes. "I kinda do. She just told him that we were brothers."

George scratched his head. "Oh yeah! My bad."

Carlos shook his head and rolled his eyes again.

"Do you want to come with us?" Ying asked.

Lang sprinted up the driveway.

Dad and Momma were at the side of the house.

Momma was washing the big bay windows.

Dad was power washing the reddish-brown bricks.

"My friends are here. Can I go with them?"

"Where?" asked Dad.

Lang shrugged.

They stopped working and marched to the end of the driveway.

They shook all the kids' hands,

and asked a bunch of questions.

Dad added all their numbers in his phone. "Have fun, son."

"Keep your cell phone on," Momma said.

"Synchronize time," his dad said. "Two hours."

Winsome Bingham

New York Times Best Books of the Year

Coretta Scott King Honor Award

Colin Bootman

Coretta Scott King Illustrator Honor Award

NAACP Image Award for Outstanding Literary Works for Children

BOOK 2 COMING IN 2024!

WELCOME TO **FORT GOODE**

WRITTEN BY WINSOME BINGHAM
ILLUSTRATED BY COLIN BOOTMAN

REYCRAFT

A veteran, Winsome Bingham has lived on Army posts like Fort Goode. Her son spent time with his friends exploring the PX, Shoppette, and the moat. Winsome writes about family, food, military life, and mental health. You can find her at binghamwrites.com.

Born in Trinidad, Colin Bootman's painting is influenced by the vibrancy of the Caribbean. At seven, he moved to the United States and later studied art and illustration. Colin has illustrated many books for children, including the Reycraft Books titles *Tapping Feet*, *Let's Draw Animals*, and *Let's Draw People*.

Welcome to Fort Goode

Lang Ford is moving, again. He's leaving his school and friends for his dad's new military post. As Lang settles into his new life and meets new friends, he learns that as long as his family is together, he is home.

Distributed by Ingram, Follett, Baker & Taylor, and Brodart

PHOTOS CREDITS: PAGE 1A: COURTESY OF W.C.H. BINGHAM; PAGE 1B: COURTESY OF COLIN BOOTMAN

@reycraftbooks

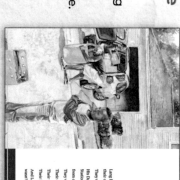

GOODE-BYE OLD

Lang Ford and his family said good-bye to their old post.

They were moving. —AGAIN

His Dad was PCS-ing, a Permanent Change of Station.

They were leaving their old post behind, from one military post to the next.

Their community.

Their work and school.

Their home.

And Lang was leaving his friends which he wasn't happy about.

5

C555

Lang pulled out his cell phone. "Time synchronized, Dad. Two hours!"

"Have fun," said Momma.

"Ditto," said Daddy.

"I will," said Lang.

"We sure will," said Carlos, snickering.

"Yep, we sure will," said George, nodding.

And they disappeared into the streets.

CO-CO-NUT!

It all happens in two weeks.

Lang is excited and anxious at the same time.

Excited to start a new school,

with new friends,

and a new teacher.

Anxious to start a new school,

with new friends,

and a new teacher.

Lang, Ying, George, and Carlos sat on the steps of the empty barracks.

Normally, Army soldiers double-timed around inside, sprinting, scurrying, scrambling,

and getting ready for formation.

But today, the unit was deployed,

off on a mission.

"I can't wait for school to start," Lang said.

"You can't?" asked Ying.

"I can," said Carlos.

"Yep. I can," said George.

Lang loved school.

He loved science and math.

He loved art and PE.

But most importantly, Lang loved food in the cafeteria and the classroom.

"I can't wait to cook in class," said Lang.

"You cooked in your class, class?" asked Ying.

"You won't do that here," Carlos said.

"Nope, not here," said George.

"Yeah, no," said Ying.

"My teacher at my last school baked brownies when we studied fractions. We made it right there in the classroom," said Lang.

Carlos shook his head.

"You won't do that here," Carlos said.

"Nope, not here," said George.

"Yeah, no," said Ying.

"Once, my teacher at my old school made a whole Thanksgiving meal in our classroom," said Lang.

"You won't do that here," Carlos said.

"Nope, not here," said George.

"Yeah, no," said Ying.

Lang laughed. "My favorite time was when she cracked a coconut. We thought milk was coming out of it."

"It didn't?" Ying asked.

Lang shook his head.

"Cracking coconuts? In the classroom?" asked Carlos.

Lang nodded.

"You won't do that here," Carlos said.

"Nope, not here," said George.

"Yeah, no," said Ying.

"So, what do you do here?" asked Lang.

"Wait, what? Milk doesn't come out of coconuts?" Ying asked.

"No. Water comes out of a coconut," said Lang.

"Water, water?" said George.

"No. Coconut water," said Lang.

"I bet he telling stories," said Carlos.

"Yep. He telling stories," said George.

"No. I'm telling the truth," said Lang.

"So, where does coconut milk comes from?" Ying asked.

"It comes from coconut. But not out of the coconut," said Lang.

Pffffft. Lang sighed.

His bottom lip trembled. "Come with me. I'll show you."

The four friends headed back to Lang's house.

Ying jumped on her skateboard.

The bros rode their bikes.

Lang's momma snapped peas on the porch.

Lang grabbed the doorknob.

"Freeze," she said.

She didn't even look up.

"Where do you think you're going?"

"I need a coconut."

Lang twisted the knob.

"Freeze," she said. "Why do you need my coconut?"

"To prove that I'm not telling stories."

Lang swung the door back.

"Freeze," she said again. "NG. No go! You're not touching my coconut."

"But, Momma, I have to prove to my friends that I'm not telling stories."

"Let me get this right," she said. "Your friends?"

She pressed her finger against her chest.

"You want to waste my good coconut and money? On a bunch of folks who think you don't tell the truth?"

George stepped behind Carlos.

He shoved Carlos forward.

"It's Carlos's fault," said George.

"You did it, too," said Carlos.

"Yeah, no," said Ying.

"And what is a coconut going to prove?" Momma asked.

"That coconuts have water inside. And not milk," said Lang.

Momma set the bowl of peas on the table.

She leaped out of the chair.

"Time to get my goggles," she said.

Lang's head dropped.

His chin touched his chest.

"Not the goggles," he said.

"Is the goggles a bad thing?" Ying asked.

"Is it?" Carlos asked.

"Yep. Is it?" George asked.

Lang's momma herded them through the door.

"Today, the goggles are a good thing," Momma said.

"She's a scientist," said Lang.

"That's cool," said George. "Our mom's a supply sergeant."

"Yep. That's cool," said Carlos.

"My mom's a lawyer," said Ying. "And a ge—Never mind."

"But I'm not a scientist today," said Momma.

"Today, I'm the coconut buster!"

She did a karate chop and a kick and a **HI-YA!**

The friends chuckled.

"And if we are going to break open coconuts, we need to protect our eyes," Momma said.

"Co-co-nut! Co-co-nut! Co-co-nut!" said the friends.

They washed their hands.

Lang gave each friend a coconut.

He grabbed a pitcher off the counter top.

Momma handed each of them a pair of goggles. "Put these on. Then meet me on the back steps."

On the back steps, they held out their coconuts.

"Co-co-nut! Co-co-nut! Co-co-nut!" they chanted.

Lang's momma reached for a coconut.

Lang stepped between his friends and his momma.

He threw his arms in the air.

"Wait. At my old school, the teacher checked with parents. To make sure no one is allergic."

"That's a great idea, baby," Momma said.

She gave Lang a fist bump.

"Okay, you hear him. Call or text whoever loves you," said Momma. "Let's go! Let's go! Let's go!"

Their fingers **TLICK-TLICK-TLICK** quickly across the screen.

"I can have coconut," said Ying.

"Me, too," said Carlos.

"Yep. Me, too," said George.

"Co-co-nut! Co-co-nut! Co-co-nut!" said the friends.

One by one, Lang's momma took a coconut from their hands.

She smashed each one against the edge of the concrete step.

CRACK!

Water gushed out.

"Wow!" said the friends.

Quickly, Lang pushed the bowl under his momma's hand.

Each coconut's water flowed into the bowl.

Broken bits of coconut laid on the steps.

Lang's momma picked up the pieces.

"What are you going to do with those?" said Ying.

"What now?" said Carlos.

"Yep. What now?" said George.

"I thought you would never ask," said Momma.

"This is my favorite, favorite, favorite part," said Lang.

They followed Momma into the kitchen.

Lang put cups on the table.

Lang's momma poured coconut water into each cup.

"I want to say something," Lang said.

Lang's momma smiled.

"Go ahead and say it, baby."

Lang raised his cup in the air.

Everyone raised their cup too.

"To my best friends. And ... you're one great momma."

"To best friends," said the friends.

Momma winked. "You're one great son."

They **GULP-GULP-GULP!** the coconut water.

Momma handed them tiny pieces of coconut.

They popped it into their mouths.

They chewed and chewed and chewed. YUM!

"That was soooooo good," said Ying.

"Really, really good," said Carlos.

"Yep. Really, really good," said George.

"You think that was good? Wait until you taste my Jamaican Grater Cake," said Momma.

And they all kept popping pieces of coconut in their mouths.

Jamaican Grater Cake

Ingredients

3 cups grated coconut

2 cups granulated sugar

1/4 cup water

1/8 teaspoon almond essence

1/4 teaspoon salt

1 teaspoon red food coloring

Directions

1) Wash and grate coconut and put to the side.

2) Mix grated coconut, granulated sugar, and water in a pot and bring to boil.

3) Turn down the fire, add in the almond essence and the salt.

4) Keep stirring until the mixture thickens up.

5) Remove 1/3 of the mixture and add a small amount of red food coloring to give it a delicate pink color.
6) Scrape remaining coconut mixture into a greased casserole dish and spread evenly.
7) Spread the pink-colored coconut over the white mixture. Let it sit for 25-30 minutes or until it's cooled.
8) Cut into squares and serve.

Preparation time: 20 minutes
Cooking time: 1 hour
Serving: 10 hungry kids

GLOSSARY

Barracks—housing for soldiers

Cargo Carrier—transport vehicle used to carry cargo

Checkpoint—a point of entry into a military installation

Chinook—heavy-lift cargo helicopter

Combat Vehicles—military vehicles used for combat operations

Military Identification Card—a card to identify military members and is needed to enter any military installation

Motorpool—a building on a military installation housing vehicles that are dispatched for use as needed

MP—military police; a police officer in the military

Permanent Change of Station (PCS)—the transfer of a military member from one duty station to the next

Sergeant First Class—military rank

Tanks—a heavy armored fighting vehicle used by the military

WINSOME BINGHAM

 is a military veteran who lived on U.S. Army posts like Fort Goode. Her son spent time with friends exploring the post's PX (Post Exchange), The Shoppette, the moat with cannons that protected the post during war time, and the woods behind the post. She is the author of *SOUL FOOD SUNDAY*, one of The New York Times Best Books of the Year. She writes about family, food, military life, and PTSD/mental health. You can find her online at binghamwrites.com.

COLIN BOOTMAN

 was born in Trinidad, where the vibrant palette of the Caribbean influenced his painting. He moved to the United States when he was seven, where he studied art and illustration. He has illustrated many books for children, winning the Coretta Scott King Illustrator Honor Award in 2004. In 2017, he won the NAACP Image Award for Outstanding Literary Works for Children. All of his award-winning illustrations show how brilliantly his art frames moments of life.